c o p p e r

graphix

AN IMPRINT OF

📖 SCHOLASTIC

New York   Toronto   London   Auckland   Sydney   Mexico City   New Delhi   Hong Kong

ISBN: 978-0-545-09892-2 (hardcover)
ISBN: 978-0-545-09893-9 (paperback)

10 9 8 7 6 5 4 3 2 1   10 11 12 13 14

First edition, January 2010
Edited by Sheila Keenan
Creative Director: David Saylor
Book design by Phil Falco
Printed in Singapore   46

CONTENTS

The *Copper* comics began life as a design for a sticker and a T-shirt. The design featured a scared little boy and his equally scared-looking dog; underneath this picture was the line "I live in a strange town."

This first *Copper* image and text was reflective of a time in my life when things weren't working out so well: My parents needed financial assistance; I lost my graphic design job; I was kicked out of my apartment; and I was attacked by a crazy guy in the street who told me to go back to my "home country," all in the span of two days. The saying "When it rains, it pours" never felt so apt.

A few months later, I snapped out of my funk and decided to pursue the career that I always felt best suited my abilities: cartooning. I had been drawing cartoons all my life, but had never committed to cartooning as a profession. All of a sudden, my cartoons mattered to me more than ever before.

I had a chance to contribute a comic to an Asian American magazine and thought back to that image of the scared boy and dog. I decided to give them names and draw a story about them. That story, "Rocket Pack Fantasy," which you can see on page 5, was the first published comic that I actually took very seriously, since I had produced mostly immature comic strips up to that point.

What had begun as a somewhat dark comic strip series quickly became more optimistic, more hopeful. The boy, Copper, was at first an observer, but by the third comic he became an active participant in his world, making choices based on his hopes and fears. Fred, the dog, was always there to question his best friend's optimism, but Copper walked ahead with his ideals, undeterred. In many ways the characters reflected my life at the time I wrote these strips, and as I look back at them I feel like I can see myself growing up. Drawing these comics gave me a sense of confidence in myself and helped me develop a sense of purpose in the work that I do. These are among the many reasons Copper and Fred hold a special place in my heart. I love these guys dearly, and I hope you enjoy their adventures as much as I have over the years.

Kazu

LOOK AT THOSE PEOPLE.

THEY ACT AS IF NOTHING EXISTS AROUND THEM.

MAYBE WE SHOULD ASK THEM WHAT THE SECRET IS.

THEY SEEM TO KNOW.

SECRET TO WHAT, FRED?

I THINK YOU JUST HAVE TO BE PATIENT FOR THE RIGHT ONE TO COME ALONG.

YOU'LL KNOW WHEN. I STILL BELIEVE THAT.

OH, C'MON!

LOOK AT US. WE'RE NOT GONNA LOOK THIS GOOD FOREVER, YOU KNOW...

I JUST GET THE FEELING WE'RE MISSING OUT...

LIKE WE'RE LETTING EVERYTHING PASS US BY...

AND IT DOESN'T HELP THAT OPPORTUNITIES NEVER PRESENT THEMSELVES.

WE JUST HAVE TO KEEP OUR EYES PEELED.

HEY, I'M WATCHING LIKE A HAWK!

EXIT

copper

THIS PLACE IS STARTING TO GET REALLY STRANGE.

STRANGE? WHAT'S SO STRANGE ABOUT WONDERFULNESS?

CASE IN POINT.

HUSH, PUPPY. WHY CRITICIZE SOMETHING YOU SIMPLY DON'T UNDERSTAND?

IN FACT, LET ME SHOW YOU JUST HOW GREAT THIS PLACE REALLY IS.

LOOK, EVEN THE SLAVES HERE ARE VERY HAPPY.

SEE?

LOOK AT ALL THE HAPPINESS! WHAT MORE COULD YOU ASK FOR?

THE SMILES ARE SIMPLY INFECTIOUS!

WHY AREN'T YOU SMILING?

GET AWAY FROM US.

IT'S YOUR DOG. HE'S MAKING YOU UNHAPPY. WE CAN TRAIN HIM TO BE BETTER.

ARF!

WHAT?! WHAT DID I DO WRONG?! LOOK AT ALL THIS GREAT STUFF I MADE FOR YOU!!!

I BUILT THIS PLACE WITH MY BARE HANDS! AND FOR WHAT?! A BRAT LIKE YOU!

C'MON, FRED!! RUN!!!

WAIT! COME BACK...

DON'T GO...

I JUST WANT YOU TO BE HAPPY.

THE KEY TO SMART SHOPPING IS TO KNOW EXACTLY WHAT YOU WANT BEFORE ENTERING THE STORE.

SEEK AND ACQUIRE. GET IN, GET OUT.

I'LL WAIT OUT HERE, THEN.

THIS'LL JUST TAKE A SEC.

WELCOME! WELCOME!

HELLO.

I'M HERE TO BUY A MAROON SCARF.

AH YES. WE HAVE THAT.

BUT MAROON IS A TERRIBLE COLOR FOR YOU, MY FRIEND.

YOU ARE A BLUE.

A BLUE?

YES, DEFINITELY.

IT WILL BRING OUT YOUR EYES.

AH, LET ME GET IT FOR YOU.

HMM, NO, SOMETHING IS MISSING. WHAT IS IT? WHAT IS IT?

AH! I KNOW WHAT IT IS! YOU ARE NOT A SCARF, BUT A HAT!

A HAT?

AH, THIS IS THE ONE.

UM, I DUNNO. IT'S A LITTLE TALL, AND EXPENSIVE.

NO! NO! IT'S THE ONE! IT IS PERFECT!

IT BRINGS OUT YOUR NOSE.

THANK YOU! THANK YOU! PLEASE COME AGAIN!

IT'S A GOOD THING YOU KNEW EXACTLY WHAT YOU WANTED. I'D IMAGINE IT'S DIFFICULT TO FIND A HAT LIKE THAT.

YEAH, IT APPARENTLY BRINGS OUT MY NOSE.

copper

WHOA WHOA HEY!

WHAT DO YOU THINK YOU'RE DOING?! THAT'S ALL MY PERSONAL STUFF!

WHY WOULD YOU NEED TO KEEP THE INSTRUCTION MANUAL FOR YOUR TOASTER?

HEY! YOU NEVER KNOW WHEN YOU MIGHT NEED IT!

WHAT IF I FORGET HOW TO USE THE FANCY TOASTING FEATURES?

YOU DON'T NEED THESE, DO YOU?

OH MAN! MY POG TOURNAMENT TROPHIES!

THAT'S MY FIRST FOOD BOWL. KEEPER, FOR SURE.

I HAVE A FEELING THIS IS GOING TO BE A PAINFUL PROCESS.

SO THAT'S WHERE I PUT MY SHARK FIN HAT...

...AFTER A LONG DAY OF TREKKING, WE'LL TREAT OUR-SELVES TO SOME MELON BREAD AT AUNT KOKO'S. THAT ALONE MAKES THE WHOLE TRIP WORTHWHILE.

AUNT KOKO

WHAT ARE YOU BUYING THOSE FOR?

I JUST REMEMBERED THAT I PROMISED AUNT KOKO I'D BRING HER SOME REDBERRIES.

UH-OH.

WHAT?

WE HAVE TO PICK UP SOME BEEF JERKY.

WHAT FOR?

FOR MARCO.

HE'S THE GUY WHO GAVE US A GREAT DEAL ON THE WINGS. HE LOVES BEEF JERKY, SO I TOLD HIM I WOULD BRING SOME BACK FROM BOLT CITY NEXT TIME WE MET...

I STILL CAN'T BELIEVE THE DEAL WE GOT ON THOSE QUALITY WINGS.

MARCO'S A GREAT GUY...

SO BUYING SOME DEHYDRATED MEAT IS THE LEAST I CAN DO.

UH-OH.

WHAT NOW?

WE HAVE TO GET SOME ION CHARGERS FOR MY FRIEND REMY...

ONE WEEK LATER...

ARE YOU READY, FRED?

READY AS I'LL EVER BE, I GUESS.

OKAY, THEN. HERE WE GO.

PUT·PUT·PUT·PUT

PUT·PUT·BLAM

WHIRRRRR

NOW WE JUST HAVE TO PICK UP SPEED!

Here I am getting ready to draw.

Behind the Scenes

In this step-by-step process section, I'll show you how I actually go about creating a *Copper* comic. The steps include:

Turning an idea into a sketch
Penciling a page based on the sketch
Inking the penciled page
Cleaning up the image
Scanning the inked page into a computer
Digitally coloring the page

The way I draw *Copper* is far different from the way I draw most of my other comics. That's because *Copper*, a complete, single-page comic, is different from my longer comic stories in the Flight or Flight Explorer anthologies or my graphic novels *Amulet* and *Daisy Kutter*. Since these comic stories are very long, I needed to find ways to quicken the pace of drawing and producing them. So I adjusted my style to suit the need for speed. I used shortcuts such as inking with a pencil instead of a pen, or scanning my sketches and using them as the pencils by printing them out very large. Anything I could do to save me time.

When I work on each *Copper* comic, however, I slow down and take my time. I use simpler methods such as limiting the use of color gradation, space, and digital color layers (*Copper* is done predominantly with simple, flat colors). I believe that limitations can be very effective in fostering creativity, and these simpler methods force me to do more with less.

This is the view from my desk. My wife, Amy, is working on her own books.

THE DRAWING BOARD

My desk is usually covered with books, movies, music, papers, pencils, and all sorts of junk. I like keeping most of my office very clean, but my desk is one place where I let loose. I love creative messes. Seeing all kinds of information around me gets my creativity flowing.

THUMBNAILS
Turning an Idea into a Story

I start by drawing a thumbnail of the *Copper* strip on a sheet of regular white paper. A thumbnail is a rough sketch version of the final comic page. In this case, I wanted to draw Copper and Fred inside of a video game, so I drew thumbnails around this simple idea. This thumbnail will be my guide as I lay out the *Copper* panels.

PANELS
Preparing the Canvas

My drawings for *Copper* are really BIG. This pad of Bristol paper is 19 by 24 inches. With a blue pencil, I draw lines to create a 15-by-15-inch square in the middle of the paper. This is the size of the final *Copper* strip. Inside this square box, I draw a line about a quarter-inch from the edge to establish the outermost panel borders.

Using my very rough thumbnail as a reference, I lay out all the panels I'll need to tell the story. These panels are not drafted to exact measurements. I just use a ruler and draw the panels to approximate sizes to save myself some time.

PENCILING
Laying the Foundation

Now we're ready to start penciling! I begin by scribbling rough versions of the images I want, and then go back to carve out all the details and solidify the shapes. I draw with a Prismacolor Col-Erase blue pencil. I find this pencil easy to use and the resulting lines easy to read. The blue color makes the lines invisible to a photocopier and can also be easily removed when scanned into a computer. Plus, it's erasable, so I don't have to worry about making mistakes.

In order to minimize the number of mistakes I make in my drawings, I use a lot of construction lines in my penciling. Construction lines are basic shapes drawn in a sketchy fashion; they're the basis for your final character and environment drawings. Construction lines are really helpful if you don't draw good shapes naturally, which I don't. I have to work hard for the image every time. In fact, whenever I sit down to work on a comic, especially *Copper*, I feel like I have to teach myself to draw all over again!

When I'm about halfway finished with the pencils, I also round the corners of the panels. For some reason, corner rounding gives me a sense of accomplishment and helps get me excited about finishing the rest of the strip.

It's all about inspiring – or tricking – yourself into getting things done. . . .

LETTERING
Putting Words in Their Mouths

The pencils are finished, the dialogue is tightened up, and I've finessed any difficult-to-manage shapes in the fine details. So I grab a 0.3 Staedtler pigment liner pen and begin lettering the comic.

I prefer to hand letter my pages because I like to have control over the composition of every image in the drawing stage. (Since dialogue takes up so much room in a panel, I treat the letters like images.) I also like hand lettering because it gives me more organic control over the volume and flow of the characters' dialogue. Along with their expressions and movements, dialogue is the major indicator of any character's "acting" on the page, so I try to liven up any scene with fun text whenever I can.

The *Copper* comics in this book, with the exception of "Lunch Pack," are hand lettered. I use a digital font made from my handwriting for longer projects such as *Amulet*.

INKING
The Old-fashioned Way

Now it's time to break out the trusty old Hunt No. 102 Crow Quill dip pen. This is one of those old-fashioned pens that you actually dip into an inkwell. If there is a pen out there with better natural line variation, I have yet to see it. The ink is Higgins Black Magic India Ink by Sanford.

The dip pen is a difficult tool to master. I started using one back when I was about 12 years old, when I discovered that it was the pen comics professionals used to ink their comics. At first, I began using it wrong! I was applying the ink from the pen with the spoon-side facing up. I kept scratching the paper and ended up with thin lines.

The correct way to use a dip pen is spoon-side down, with the ink on it facing the paper. I know this seems dangerous, but don't worry. If used correctly, the ink will flow through the pen tip and not simply spill off and spoil your page.

After many years of breaking pen nibs, spilling ink, and ruining drawings, I've finally become comfortable with this old-fashioned tool, and I'm really quite fond of it. If you plan to use a nib pen, be sure to start early!

I make my way down the page, moving from left to right as I ink. I don't necessarily follow the panels in reading order. I go whichever way guarantees I won't run my drawing hand over any wet ink. With a dip pen, the ink dries very slowly. Only a few years ago, this page would have been covered in Wite-Out correction fluid to patch up all the smears left by my hand. Today, I'm much more adept because I've inked so many drawings, and now I rarely smudge the ink.

GOING DIGITAL
Technology as a Paintbrush

Once I put the old-school pen and ink away, things get a little advanced. You may not need all of this technology to create your own fine comic strip, but these digital tools do a lot to help me bring a professional level of finish to my comics. Coloring using the computer allows for tons of flexibility in the editing process and nearly all final files used for print production are digital nowadays.

For the digital part of the *Copper* process, I use a:

    Computer
    Scanner
    Drawing Tablet
    Adobe Photoshop

My computer is hooked up to a tablet screen and also a regular drawing tablet. A tablet is a tool that allows the user to draw on the computer. While the tablet screen allows me to draw directly on the screen, the regular tablet allows me to draw without my hand getting in the way of my view. Both tablets have their advantages, and I enjoy using both for different projects. However, the regular tablet can be purchased for a modest price (some cost less than a hundred dollars), while the screen is very expensive. I recommend using a simple, cheap tablet to begin with. I got my first by trading away a video game system!

Adobe Photoshop is the computer software I use to color all of my comics. It is an incredibly powerful piece of software that most professionals use to create and touch up images.

Here we begin the digital part of the process by scanning the comic into the computer. I currently use a large-format scanner to scan my comics. This is a luxury I was not able to afford until recently. For most of my career, I used small, cheap scanners purchased at the local electronics store. I used to have to scan the *Copper* comics in six separate parts and then piece them together in the computer. Now, I only need to stitch together two pieces! This saves me a lot of time. However, the cheaper, smaller scanners and a little extra patience will do the job just fine. I scan the comic at 300 DPI or higher to make sure I have enough information to make the files read clearly when printed. "DPI" stands for "dots per inch" and represents the density of the information being scanned. The higher the DPI is, the sharper the image will look.

COLORING
The Magic of Digital Paint

This is the comic after it has been scanned into the computer and pieced together to form one image. It is now a Photoshop file and I can begin to work on it digitally.

Using the Hue/Saturation and Level adjusts, I can cancel out the blue lines and the paper texture, cleaning the image and leaving me with only the black lines to work with.

The linework is left on its own layer, set to multiply (which allows you to see through the white portions of the page), and I will begin painting on separate layers underneath the linework.

I start by selecting the panels and coloring them with a neutral value. An example of a neutral value is the color gray, since it is lighter than black and darker than white. It is helpful to begin with this neutral color and add to it rather than to just drop different colors onto the white page. This allows for the color palette of the entire piece to remain balanced and cohesive. Painters call this applying a "key" color to the image. In this case, I chose a tan color to work from. The dialogue bubbles are kept white, so they are easy to read.

The next step is to color the characters and objects, setting them on separate layers for easy adjustment. While Copper and Fred have a designated set of colors, everything else around them is fair game for adjustment. The only rule is to make sure all the colors look good together. Easier said than done.

The characters and objects are painted with simple colors first, and on their own layers. These will provide the base for the comic's final color palette.

Since I am using only flat colors, I can easily select the individual colors and change them using tools like the Hue/Saturation adjust. I spend a lot of time messing around with the colors to get the comic to look just right. This process is kind of like choosing clothes to wear for the day. Sometimes it can take forever!

Here I have shifted the background panels to cooler colors using the Hue/Saturation adjust. I found that these cooler colors better fit the blue of the characters' armor. The green color is a mix of the tan color established above and the cooler blues of the armor. Having an understanding of how colors mix together is very helpful at this point, and one of the great things about working in digital media is the ability to test out various color combinations to see what happens. Before working on the computer, I never formally learned to paint or use color, but now I feel I have a good grasp of colors and basic painting techniques.

In most cases, I focus on one panel at the beginning, and get the colors just right for that panel. That way, I can use this fully colored panel as a guide for the rest of the comic. Once a color is selected for a particular item, like the armor, I can just apply that same color to the armor in each of the rest of the panels and save myself a lot of time.

On this comic strip, I decided to use effects layers. By applying a solid orange color on the characters' faces on a separate layer and turning the layer transparent, I create the illusion of a clear mask on the helmet. An effect layer is also applied to the background to create the illusion of shadows. This can be seen in the darker greenish hues on the backgrounds of the version below. Tricks like these can add depth to the images.

In the later stages of the coloring process, I add highlights to the characters and backgrounds to indicate the lighting in the scene. Putting a lighter blue on the tops of the helmets and armor really helps give the comic a sense of space.

While it may seem easy to do, the coloring process actually takes quite a while. This is a good chance for me to listen to music or an audiobook while I work, and I usually have a lot of fun during the process.

Here is the finished product. If I did my job correctly, the reader will not be thinking too much about the making of *Copper* and will simply enjoy this story.

I hope this step-by-step was helpful and informative for all you budding cartoonists. We can never have enough good cartoonists in the world, since everybody loves cartoons, don't they? Good luck on your fantastic creations and thanks for reading this book!

ACKNOWLEDGMENTS

I'd like to thank my wife, Amy, and my assistants, Anthony Wu, Jason Caffoe, and Stuart Livingston, for helping me put together this book. Anthony and Jason did a wonderful job coloring the "Lunch Pack" story, and Stuart helped flatten some of the single-page comics. Amy helped with the organization and formatting of files, and has provided love and support throughout my career in comics.

Thanks, you guys. I couldn't possibly have done this without you!

OTHER GRAPHIC NOVELS BY KAZU KIBUISHI

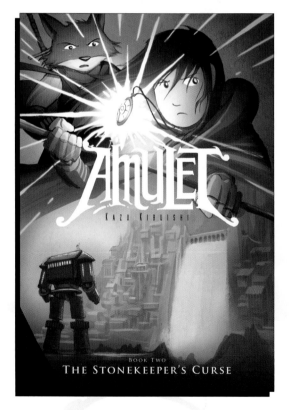